For all the strays

About This Book

The illustrations for this book were done in oil paint on board with hand-cut paper and Photoshop. This book was edited by Christy Ottaviano and designed by Angelie Yap. The production was supervised by Lillian Sun, and the production editor was Jen Graham. The text was set in Bliss Pro, and the display type is hand lettered.

First Edition: June 2022 • Christy Ottaviano Books is an imprint of Little, Brown and Company. The Christy Ottaviano Books name and logo are trademarks of Hachette Book Group, Inc. • The publisher is not responsible for websites (or their content) that are not owned by the publisher. • Library of Congress Cataloging-in-Publication Data • Names: Hemingway, Edward, author, illustrator. • Title: Pigeon and Cat / Edward Hemingway. • Description: First edition. | New York : Little, Brown and Company, 2022. | "Christy Ottaviano Books." | Audience: Ages 4–8. | Summary: Cat and Pigeon live in a city lot, and while they do not have much, they have each other, so when Pigeon goes missing after a storm, Cat leaves the safety of their lot for the first time and traverses the city looking for her. • Identifiers: LCCN 2021012398 | ISBN 9780316311250 (hardcover) • Subjects: CYAC: Friendship—Fiction. | Cats—Fiction. | Pigeons—Fiction. • Classification: LCC PZ7.H377436 Pi 2022 | DDC [E]—dc23 • LC record available at https://lccn.loc.gov/2021012398 • ISBN 978-0-316-31125-0 • PRINTED IN CHINA • APS • 10 9 8 7 6 5 4 3 2 1

Pigeon & Cat

EDWARD HEMINGWAY

Christy Ottaviano Books

LITTLE, BROWN AND COMPANY
New York Boston

In an abandoned city lot
there sits a cardboard box.
Inside the box lives Cat.

The box is old and battered, but it keeps Cat warm when it's cold and dry when it's wet. It's filled with his scant possessions:

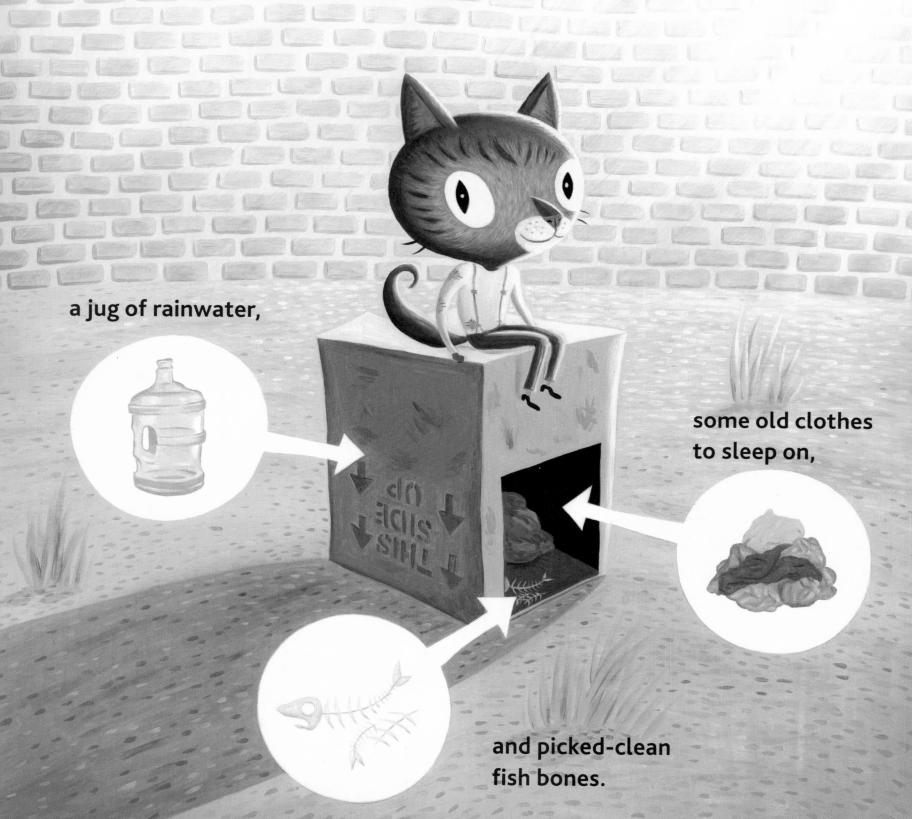

a jug of rainwater,

some old clothes to sleep on,

and picked-clean fish bones.

When Cat's hungry, he scales the fence to scavenge for food in the trash bins on the sidewalk. It's the only time he ever leaves the lot.

After eating his fill, he returns to his box and takes a catnap with one eye open.

That way, if any of the other neighborhood strays climb over the fence to lie in the shade of a tree or bask in bits of sunlight on the crabgrass, Cat is ready. He shows his claws, hisses loudly, and drives them off.

The lot isn't much, but it's his home *and his alone*.
It's been this way for as long as Cat can remember.

Then one windy night Cat spots an overturned nest near a window ledge. Looking closely, he finds an unbroken egg inside. White as fish bone and warm as summer rain, it's too beautiful to eat.

Peck.
Peck.
Crack!

Cat carefully picks it up and brings it to his box. He watches in wonder as a tiny hatchling pecks her way out of the shell.

Cat welcomes the little bird into the world.

Hello there, Pigeon!

His new friend responds in her own special way.

Cat searches the trash bins for something tasty to give the tiny bird, and soon Pigeon is eating from Cat's paw.

She fits perfectly on his lap.

Safely tucked away together in his box, Cat naps to Pigeon's first birdsong.

In time, and under Cat's care,
Pigeon grows strong.

Soon she finds her wings and flies to the top of the lot.

The city beyond is full of bright colors, lights, and sounds.

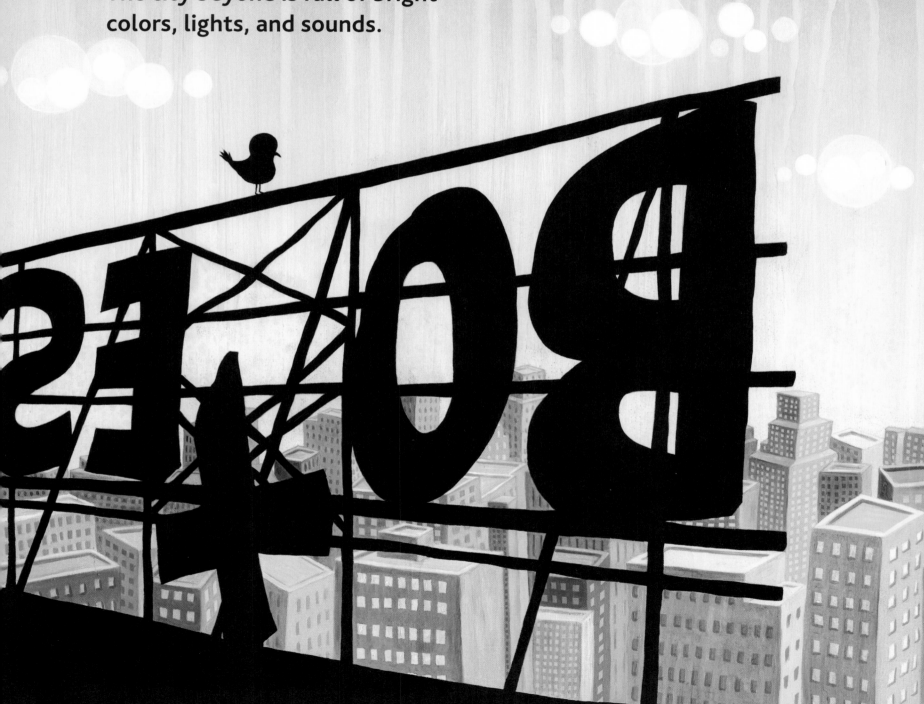

When Pigeon returns a little later, she has a bright red piece of chalk in her beak for Cat.

It's the nicest gift he's ever received.

The next day, and every day that follows, Pigeon searches for colorful discarded treasures in the city for Cat.

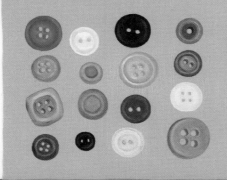

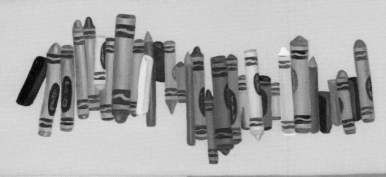

Pigeon's bright gifts light Cat's imagination, and what starts as a small spark inside him grows into a glowing fire.

Cat doesn't want to keep this new warmth to himself, so he rolls up his sleeves and begins to transform a wall in the lot into something beautiful.

But one dark afternoon Pigeon doesn't return from treasure hunting.
Cat stands vigil, looking into the angry sky until he's forced to hide
from the rain and wind.

When the storm passes, he calls out for his friend till
his voice is hoarse. Pigeon is nowhere to be found.

The lot isn't much, but it's become *nothing* without Pigeon. Gathering all his courage and some possessions, Cat climbs over the fence and into the city.

Using the chalk she gave him,
Cat leaves messages for Pigeon.
Soon they dot the walls, streets,
and sidewalks around him.

With every new message that Cat makes, the city looks a little more like home. Had he really been afraid of this world beyond his lot? It's not so bad.

And that night, for the very first time, Cat forgets to nap with one eye open.

Days turn into weeks. Other strays cross Cat's path, but he doesn't show his claws or hiss loudly. Instead, he smiles and asks if they've seen Pigeon.

When they say no, he shares his smelly fish heads with them.

Now and again, he gives them bright little gifts of their own.

Pigeon might be lost to Cat, but in this small way he feels as close to her as ever.

Then one day he sees a flock of birds carrying something colorful in their beaks. Cat follows the birds, and soon they lead him to a strangely familiar place.

It's his old lot, and
PIGEON IS THERE!

Pigeon tells Cat how she injured her wing in the storm...and slowly made her way back

(after many, many days) to the lot.   But Cat was gone.   !!!   While she waited for him

(and with the help of the animals in the neighborhood),   Pigeon opened the lot to all the strays.

She hopes Cat doesn't mind.*   * Translation

Oh, Pigeon,
how could
I mind?

"We've always understood each other."

That very night Cat joins the animals
in the shelter for a celebration dinner.
Pigeon still fits perfectly on his lap.

In a bustling city lot there is a shelter filled with animals, light, art, and laughter. ALL ARE WELCOME.

It's been this way for as long as Pigeon and Cat can remember.

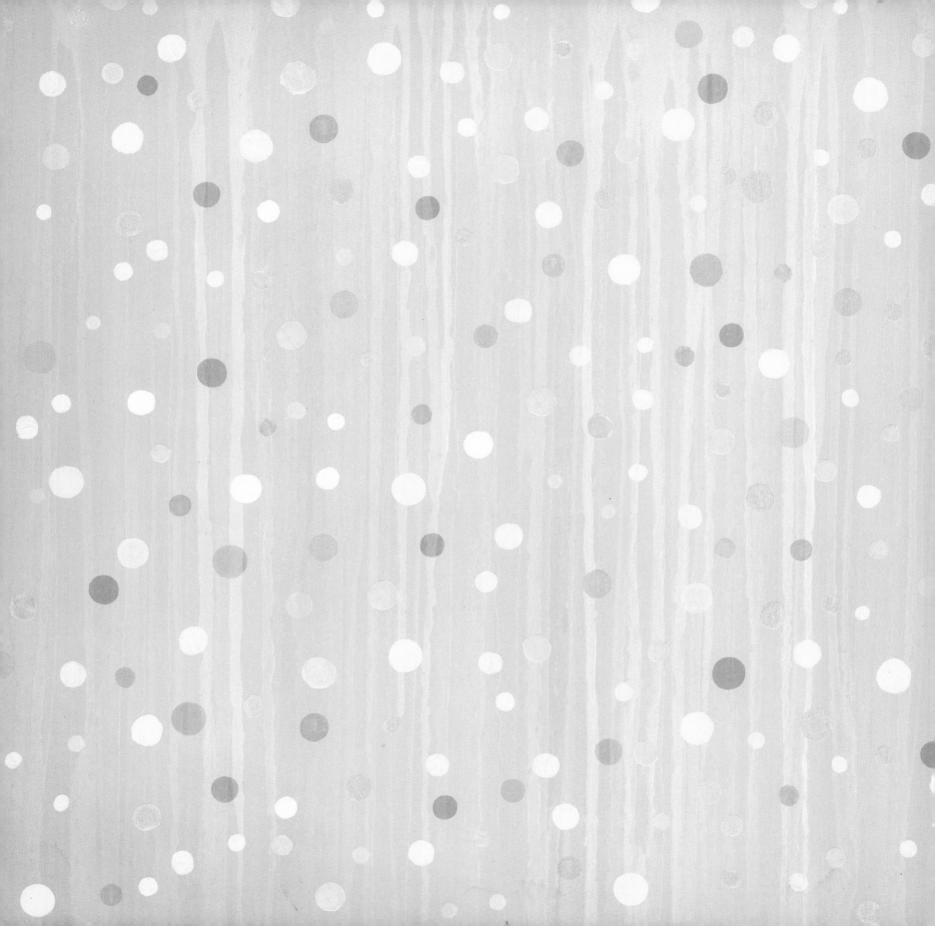